Thick City

Thick City

Katie Jean Shinkle

BULL • CITY
PRESS

DURHAM, NORTH CAROLINA

Thick City

Library of Congress Cataloging-in-Publication Data

Names: Shinkle, Katie Jean, author.
Title: Thick city / Katie Jean Shinkle.
Description: Durham, North Carolina : Bull City Press, [2022]
Identifiers: LCCN 2022033463 (print) | LCCN 2022033464 (ebook) |
ISBN 9781949344394 (paperback) | ISBN 9781949344400 (ebook)
Subjects: LCGFT: Novels.
Classification: LCC PS3619.H5766 T48 2022 (print) |
LCC PS3619.H5766 (ebook) | DDC 813/.6--dc23/eng/20220721
LC record available at https://lccn.loc.gov/2022033463
LC ebook record available at https://lccn.loc.gov/2022033464

Published in the United States of America

Book design by Spock and Associates

Cover design by Savannah Bradley
Author photo by PJ Carlisle

Published by BULL CITY PRESS
1217 Odyssey Drive
Durham, NC 27713
www.BullCityPress.com

Contents

Thick City

Our mothers show us how to pull the bodies out from underneath the beds. It's not really cleaning, they tell us, if you only shove things around. You have to fold and put away, fold and put away; everything has a place where everything belongs. Putting things in their places is a talent we do not possess. Our mothers open a cupboard with shelves and say fold the body into a square, head tucked to chest, legs and arms crisscrossing. Instead, we take the bodies in handfuls and stuff them under the bed. We cannot understand how shapes fit within the confines of other shapes and that, in itself, is hard to accept. We don't want to move on to scrubbing the blood in the toilet. We get under the bed, too. We have snuck the red, white, and blue popsicles we are not supposed to be eating. We crack them into fingers, they grow from our hands. We chomp the freezer-burned tops with our back teeth. One day we will no longer fit under the bed. We will be folded into squares, put away. Our paychecks this week will go to replenishing popsicles.

Meanwhile, a forefinger coming down on a small ant on a desk, killing and smearing. The crack of an egg. White jeans snapping in hot, dry wind. The whine of a table saw. Two people at the end of a driveway talking with their hands, laughing silent laughs. Beyond them, children in a living room of a split-level house ramming a toy car into a larger pile of toy cars. In the distance, the continuous beeping of the drawbridge stuck for the fifth hour, car horns talking, too, with their hands, balled fists waving over steering wheels, someone is coming to fix it soon. Through the walls next door, the baby is crying. His mother is single, but looking, or so says her dating app profile. She doesn't tell anyone about him, too scared of outright rejection. She wants a woman who will accept her for who she is, but not too much of who she is. How to explain to a single, twentysomething, butch woman that she has a baby? It's too complex, really, she thinks, as she pulls her nipple out of her shirt, folds it like an envelope as her midwife showed her, and gently delivers it to the already gripping baby's mouth. He latches, pulls, drinks. She likes to pat her hand on his stomach to feel it filling it up with slow, methodical expansion like a water balloon. The cries are so distant sometimes, from elsewhere, the baby doesn't seem real. On the other side of the wall, I face a plate filled with a whole dried salmon (head attached); sweet cherries (pitted); a small salad of arugula and black olives (no dressing). Hands over my ears, I stare into the salmon's hollow face. It turns its head, opens its mouth, and out comes the baby's cry. I punch the salmon's head back down with my fist. I think of my own dating profile, the one I made behind my partner's back. How, I, too am looking. There is no heart here at home. What ship long sailed. I am alone with my crying fish, my fruits, my sad salad. Maybe I need a baby. Maybe, in the night, I should steal the baby next door, let his mother find her own butch to run away with. Maybe I should give her mine. The crying intensifies, through the walls, on my dinner plate. I grab a blanket from the couch. I wrap the fish in it, push the cherries around the head, shape the salad into a tidy diaper on the bottom. I swaddle my food baby until all I see is the gaping mouth of the salmon's head. I unbutton my shirt, bring my left breast out of my bra. I fold my nipple into the salmon's mouth.

Meanwhile, the sun visor's mirror dips her lettuce hair into view. Coley scoops it into a top-knot salad, the messier the best. She is finicky about how much the ends look tossed precisely so. A spectacle of prepackaged manufacturing, yet it has to look organic. She uses licked fingers to force flyaways in every direction. Must look exerted. Natural. No effort, all effort.

She slaps the sun visor up, sits in dawn twilight, adjusts the ring light behind her which gives the illusion her cheekbones are more angular so she doesn't have to suck in as much, purse her lips as often.

A few minutes before, she opened her throat and slammed down to the top of the label a two-liter of Coca-Cola and then slowly replaced the liquid with a half-pint of Johnnie Walker Black. She loves watching the golden liquid coat the inside of the plastic, rounding every curve of the bottle like a wave. A loud screeching outside of the car makes her jump and her thighs involuntarily squeeze the newly full, uncapped two-liter between them, spewing booze and soda all over her leggings, her car seat, her steering wheel. She doesn't react much beyond a cringe. She takes a long drink from the bottle to compose herself, suckling the ridged top with her lips, running her tongue mindlessly inside the smoothness of the corrugated opening. The world at this hour is horizon-full and almost shadow empty. She only has a short window of time before the sun will be fully up and her own natural movie set will vanish.

There is a kind of geometry to this light, she thinks, when the gradations feel rapturous, all-encompassing. Like when Mr. Schwinn drew on the board in middle school art class to teach about shading and dimension. She felt like she could live inside of his drawings and stay there, in the light and depth, down the streets and in the mansions that were better and bigger than where any of them lived. She remembered, then, how she had convinced everyone in class she was rich and lived in a house with ten bathrooms. Nina D., who lived next door, thank god, went along with her lies, though later blackmailed her. As payment to keep her secret, Nina made Coley call her on Saturday morning for "beauty tips," saying she needed them. Nina lived for adoration, but rarely received it. When Coley called, Nina told her to drink more water, which wasn't bad advice, considering, but certainly not the beauty tip she was hoping to hear. Coley wanted Nina's secret map of how desire worked, the ways in which she could hold it in her hands and mold it, draw point A to B and go there. The light outside roils along the tops of the trees, threatens to burst through in oranges and pinks at any minute. She's losing her moment.

Coley dips a handkerchief into the whiskey and Coke, soaks it, and puts it to her forehead, to the back of her neck, to her collarbone. She soaks it and dabs her hair. She squeezes the brown, sticky liquid underneath her armpits, squeezes it above her sports bra and runner's tank top of the same material. Everything must look damp. She must have beads of moisture in some places, and pools of moisture in other places. She must look like she sweated hard, but not so hard as to be unpleasant.

She wrings out more liquid onto the bottom of her tank top. There is almost too much light, so she has to hurry. She takes out her phone and starts the video. "Hey Team Let's Do It! What a great day! Rise and shine! Smashed my workout, and oh babes, I feel soooo good! I didn't want to come in today, I wasn't feeling it, wanted to stay in bed! But wow, I'm so glad I got to the gym and worked those feelings alllll the way out! Remember: no one is going to clap for you, you have to clap for your own self! Show up and try! Never give up! Do it for you and no one else! You got this! Don't forget today is the last day for twenty-five percent off my customized fitness plan with code LETSDOIT. Love you!"

Her phone clicks to indicate the video has stopped, she uploads to her feed, her story, and closes the app. She takes slug after slug from the two-liter, shuts her eyes, imagines God breastfeeding her, huge hands nestle and cradle. She finally takes a breath, wipes her mouth on her forearm, opens the window, and dumps out the rest of the whiskey and Coke, splashing her car door. She throws the bottle on the ground, partially rolls her window up. The world is in full-on morning. She is almost in a full-on panic. She lights the bottom of a small, bulbous, glass pipe, sucks and exhales thick yellow smoke that mostly fills the car, but also leaks languidly into the air outside. She leans her head on the steering wheel, sets the pipe in her cupholder. The notifications pile up: red hearts and hashtags, a chorus of agreement, #girlswhodieforhealth, #bodybaggoals, #deathmotivation, which rise from her phone's screen out of focus and dripping. She lights a cigarette, the gas station's neon Lagunitas beer sign is all fritz and blink. Beyond the sign, inside the gas station, the young man behind the counter smiles while counting money from the drawer. Almost shift change. Miguel, he's practically a friend at this point. Here is everything she knows about him: He is working on his degree in Materials Science and Engineering at the university downtown, lives at home to cut costs even though his parents have said they will pay for housing. He likes living at home. Still has a brother in high school, and they are close. He likes his family. He likes the gas station. He likes his classes. He's a very good student. He's going to be a very good engineer. Here is everything he knows about her: nothing. She watches him run his fingers through his swoopy bangs in flirtation at a customer she cannot see, this time the creases around his mouth look concerned, in an ohhh instead of an ahhhh. She stubs her cigarette out into the cupholder. She doesn't even attempt to slice the smoke with her hand to clear it.

Her clothes are dry, it happened so quickly. Her face is too, for the most part, except her dirty scalp and shredded lettuce tendrils, which are wilted and rotten. She takes a giant bite from a king-sized KitKat she always buys from Miguel before she makes her daily workout video, her only meal of the day. The chocolate tastes like chemicals on her tongue. She has a moment of clarity—*all the candy in the gas station is poison, the government is poisoning us*—and spits the mouthful on the floor mat. She regrets throwing the whiskey away. When she backs her car out, she hears the plastic bottle crush underneath the tires.

Meanwhile, what does she taste like after all? More like mint & calendula & nasturtiums & lavender in November fog, the kind like in movies set in England or swimming under the cobble-pebble lake trestle?

Her taste on your lips. You are intimately aware of what she does, and how she does it. She is, after all, your very favorite. But then, there are those times. "Why do you always act surprised?" she says. Here, you want to jump through the screen, strangle the sweaty, hairy man with the tinted sunglasses. He's the one who puts his hands down the front of her shirt first, and at 28:12 is from behind initiating a scene ending at 43:57 with a double money shot down the curves of her waist. These videos inspire love, and envy, in you. You want to pull her off the leather couch, tell all those people they don't deserve her.

She is a star at Dangling Willy's. She transforms into VERONICA!!! The voice echoes in an auto-tuned twang. Hair extensions, false eyelashes, contouring, nipple pasties, the waves of creation. VERONICA!!!

dances to Master P, DMX, and Montell Jordan in rotation and exclusively. On your birthday you get her to dance to "the biggest cliché of her life" she says, a Nine Inch Nails song, fulfilling a pathetic teenage fantasy from 1994.

And while you are in love, you wait until she is asleep to talk to the Other: "Sir," you whisper into your phone. "How will you feed me?" Sir doesn't want to hear about your pedestrian Fiesta dinnerware fantasies. He knows you like your kibble from a bowl on the floor. "Take your clothes off," Sir says. Even over the phone, you comply. You obey.

The next day, you wake late in the afternoon. VERONICA!!! has gone to work. You have many missed calls. Sir is reciting esoteric poetry. This is how you both communicate your wants and needs. Through lines you recall unsafe things, relay defining moments, moments you carry in your heart: once, at the absolute peak of loneliness, before VERONICA!!!, before Sir, you let two men you met from the internet spit on and hit you, and after the hookup, for which you paid, you went to the mall to buy cologne. How some teenagers were driving erratically in front of you, so you laid on your horn. How when you finally parked, they circled the lot until you got out of your car. How they looked confused and yelled, "Fuck you, fat ass faggot!" How you never entered the building. How you went home and stared at a wall for an hour. You didn't leave your house for another week.

Once you get home from walking around the city, from throwing your phone in an uptown garbage can,

VERONICA!!! is asleep in the king-size bed tucked neatly under a nude painting of herself. Before you threw your phone away, you wrote to Sir: let's meet, please, we must, or I'll die. You couldn't bring yourself to go through with it. You walked right past his building as he watched you from the window.

Meanwhile, with our paychecks, we are at Pets 4 Less watching a calico rat choke on a piece of food. We want to adopt it, name it Wrench. An aisle over, we hear them: "Tell me what her name is! Tell me who it was! Why won't you tell me who you slept with?" We are in the back of the store, but we can still feel the thunder when it cracks outside.

Meanwhile, in a big house on the shoreline, Shanice stands behind the couch and folds her body forward from the waist, letting the weight of her neck and head dangle, placing her hands on the floor, her ten-carat diamond ring shiny, sending pockets of shimmer onto the walls where the sun hits. She sways gently, cradling her elbows with her hands. She pedals her heels. As soon as the blood has pooled into her head, she stands up quickly. She loves the rush, the slight jolt. She does this again: forward fold, blood rush. When the jolt becomes tiresome, she paces. She watches the television as big as a billboard. The show goes a little something like this:

Step One: The prosecutor states a fact and asks a question.

Step Two: The defense shrugs and sighs.

Step Three: The prosecutor calls witness after witness, hears testimony after testimony.

Step Four: The defense rests.

Shanice stops pacing, sits in the middle of the sprawling purple couch. She can see herself reflected when the screen goes black. She takes a tissue from the inside band of her yoga pants and wrings it between her fingers. The reflected scene of her on the couch almost looks normal, as if everything is as it should be, and always has been. Pictures on the walls above her of her daughter, tall and long lashed, buoyant and gay. Shanice loves her. She had come out to them as gay a few weeks earlier. Now, she has a girlfriend named Maureena. Maureena is a newly retired teen actress, a "Scream Queen" she is called because of her exhaustive résumé of B-list horror films.

When the commercials end, there is her daughter in the courtroom. Shanice's grief is so deep it cannot touch her daughter's name without overflowing her body. The camera darts awkwardly to the face of the judge, then pans to the face of her husband, then to their attorney, and then back to the judge. Their daughter is in the background, no longer in view. Shanice can hear a woman crying. The judge clears his throat into his microphone and pauses.

Across the bottom of the screen reads: Thick City Teen's Family Wins Overdose Case.

Their daughter's new girlfriend stole Shanice's OxyContin from the knee surgery she'd had years ago. She forgot the bottles were even in the drawer.

The screen goes dark.

Shanice screams.

Meanwhile, my ex-girlfriend, R, and I finish our relationship like this: five bamboo plants I gave her as gifts left outside on the doorstep of my new apartment. When asked why she left them plants, she says, "Because *fuck you* that's why."

A pool party on the top deck of our old apartment building that will burn down soon, though we don't know this yet. When the pool party begins, the water is too cold so no one is swimming, everyone loafing around longingly gazing at the water. –Someone will drown tonight—I tell R.

I am ending our relationship with a pool party and a prediction. The worst thing: two drunk people get locked out of the building, have to sleep in Adirondack chairs.

There is a note on the new door to my new apartment in R's handwriting: "Who was your New Year's kiss?" The note is not meant for me but for my new roommate. The handwriting is not R's but someone else's, a forgery, a thin disguise. *Who was your New Year's kiss?* –It certainly wasn't me—I say aloud to the note, which is lineated like poetry, taped with Christmas-themed gift-wrapping tape, all pine trees and golden garlands.

A few months ago, R and I were driving toward the mountains and the mountains were on fire. At a certain point, under an overpass on a one-way dwindling road, we were stopped by the authorities, large men in huge gas masks, and were told to turn right around, the fire is spreading quickly, get away from this place, you don't belong here.

But here was where the scene doubles back. Here was R in the moment before our apartment catches on fire. Here was R taking over the wheel as I passed out behind it on the mountain's gradually thinning road just before we were asked to turn around.

R says she is a power bottom, and I am aware by the way she says yes, yes, when I am on top of her, yes, yes. When I say –yes, sir—I mean it. "Don't call me sir, it drives me nuts, especially when you say it in public," she says. When we are on the train, we see a mistress and a submissive acting out a power dynamic and I nod to R and say –see—see—do you see what I see—you see—.

Our world was ending and R said, "I am taking you to the mountains to break up with you. Pets 4 Less is no place to end things." We were using her new girlfriend's car, but I did not know this yet, I did not know she had a new girlfriend. –You don't have to drive me to the mountains to tell me anything—I said. When we drove back from the mountains, the apartment was on fire.

I am in my new apartment by myself. R wants to come over and I let her and within an hour my fist is in her mouth. I try calling her a dirty little slut. –Talk to me, you little slut, tell me how you like it—and she pauses. "Who said you could call me a slut?" she says. The words echo and the echoes become echoes until echoes are not enough, never enough. I call her a slut and she stops moaning, moving, breathing, all her air is choked as if caught inside of her. –What happened—I'm sorry—are you OK—I'm sorry—is everything OK—I'm sorry—hello—hello—talk to me—I say. An hour later, she is gone again.

When I first met R, she almost stopped talking to me when she heard the kind of films I like to watch. She is very picky about these types of things. "Have you seen this film? That film?" she asked, and I said –no—and somehow, still to this day, I am ashamed I haven't been pickier about my film choices. "It was almost a deal breaker," she said.

R was leaving me to a soundtrack; a soundtrack differing greatly from the soundtrack of our lives. How music I never thought I would hear was playing itself throughout our apartment, an apartment about to burn to the ground. R was listening to The Who's *Tommy*. "I love Tina Turner in this film," she said. And then, looking sideways at me, "Oh, you've never seen it, I forgot."

One by one the bamboo plants show up outside the door. I don't know where R is, and I can no longer ask who she is with or what she is doing because it is no longer any of my business.

We were sitting on the corner of the street, our apartment building on fire, and everything she owned was gone. She wanted me to drink her blood. There was an explosion. Her body was bloody and she offered her arm and said, "Lick it." She smashed her open wound into mine. My knees were scraped and bleeding, too. "Together forever," she said.

But we will not be together forever. We were on top of the mountain and she said, "No, no, no, it's all wrong, this is too much, too intense, we have to end." –I haven't even given you much intensity—I said to the trees, to the mountains. R was no longer listening. "There is a possessiveness here I cannot wrap my head around, and I can no longer go there with you," she said. She was the largest tree in the forest. She was a tree split two ways, an opening so large you can drive a car through. We were driving her new girlfriend's car through the gigantic hole in the tree. We were driving through and I wanted to get out of the new girlfriend's car and take a picture. I wanted to look up inside the innards together, what guts. I wanted to take a picture of us inside of the gigantic opening in this tree in the middle of my heartbreak. She refused to take a picture with me.

Meanwhile, talk about a bundle of hair and bone, teeth/blood/bow-tied with a ligament, what looks like cartilage from a neck of a chicken, two-toned in its translucence. This bundle is in the toilet but where did it come from?

Dani and her boyfriend smoke shards out of a broken light bulb, what looks like golden glass from a stained-glass window, a color also seen in the framed pictures on the walls of the Planned Parenthood clinic downtown. Dani shared needles only once when she was a kid, she said, but got over that right quick after a stint in a halfway house full of nut jobs, mouth breathers, and zombie freaks, all whacked out on psych meds worse than dope. "I'd shoot all the dope in the world to not be a mouth-breather zombie freak all whacked out on their anti-whatevers," Dani says, taking a quick inhale of smoke and coughing.

Ash leaves her and barricades himself in the bathroom. He stares at the bundle of tooth, blood, and vein. He says, "Could this have come out of me?" He begins to rip into his own arms with an X-ACTO knife. "Where is the bone?" he says. His muscles are shiny. "Your bones are in your body, you don't have to see them, I promise they are there," Dani says through the door.

The mass floats in the toilet water for days. After Ash gets his arms sutured up as dark as tattoos, steel stitches he will later pluck out one-by-one with pliers, zigzag, zigzag, the mass turns from dark to light, shrinks and contracts, bubbles and swirls until an overlapping separation forms between bone, hair, blood, outlined in silver, connected as if through a Venn diagram.

Dani says, "I don't think it came from me." They are breaking a new light bulb against the wall, they are inhaling, exhaling, coughing. "All my insides are rotten," she says, "and all my insides fell out long ago."

Meanwhile, the sign inside the children's section says PETRI IS GONE (BUT NOT FORGOTTEN!) HE WAS A GOOD FRIEND. CHECK BACK IN AUGUST FOR A NEW FRIEND. The home of Petri is taken from the front and brought to the back, out of sight, but the smell from the cage lingers of cedar and mustiness. If only making friends were so easy, I think. Lose a friend, get a new one. Misplace one, here's another one. May I offer you a Friendship Menu where you can pick and choose your desired traits for this new, improved friend? Today's special is Compassion, Kindness, and Loyalty. I think of a friend in college, a bit of a narcissist, a bit of a sociopath asking me, "How do you make friends?" A quite masterful exclusion, chiseling a crack right through what I considered a shared, intimate moment. Are we not friends if you must ask such a question? I still think of this question from time to time, "How do you make friends?" coming from a supposed friend. And of course, with the lingering-wood-chip-turned-shit-trap in the air, I consider the question once more. Was Petri a friend? My friend? A *good* one, even? What did he ever do for me? I fed him. I held him. The wailing begins. One wailing child, forlorn when they realize the cage is gone, small chubby fists hitting the floor, Petri!!! The swollen face of agony. Another. Another. All day long, wailing children.

My ex-girlfriend is no longer my friend or she is, ostensibly, another bad friend. Terrible, in fact. There are times when I believe we were never friends at all.

What friendship traits off of the Friendship Menu would I have selected had I the option then? Empathy? Integrity? Thoughtfulness? Love?

The last time a pet from the children's section died, we were still together.

"How was your day?" my then-girlfriend, now ex-girlfriend, asked.

"The pet friend died at the bookstore," I said. "The one in the children's section."

"No big deal, I'm sure they will get another one," she said. "What do gerbils cost, like two dollars? Who cares."

"Sparky was a rat," I said.

I did not ask her about her day because suddenly I did not care about her day anymore. She lifted her massive mixing bowl and long wooden ladle from the bedside stand. She ate all of her meals in bed. She never made anything for me. She set the bowl and ladle on the counter next to the sink, and not in the sink, and she certainly never attempted to clean or fold or put things away.

Today, the bedroom is dank, blackout curtains pulled tight when I enter to go to bed. I don't eat dinner. I am still thinking about Petri, the smell of cedar chips in my hair, the residue of friendship left behind. How dispensable and tenuous a heart the size of a pea can be. I get under the covers and put my arm where my ex-girlfriend would have been. Instead of her rounded stomach, her flat hips, I cradle balls of fur, so many, and all of them moving at once. A body made of fur balls, bone, and teeth. One crawls into my cupped hand and falls asleep—I can feel its rapid heartbeat against my fingertips.

₪

Meanwhile, in the park this morning, we pass the woman with a stroller. She, a regular, is on the same bench at the same hour every single day. A few minutes later, she run-walks in one-minute intervals around the park, pushing the stroller, cooing into the basket, singing, "Mommy's here, mommy cares, mommy loves you," baritone and rich. Today is the first time we notice her stroller is empty.

Meanwhile, Annie and the telephone bill are driving across town to retrieve her daughter from soccer practice, top speed, screeching tires. She doesn't turn her headlights on. She parks and stands at the edge of the field, watching girls with short legs kick and follow a ball, as if in slow motion. There is a whistle, the coach yells, "That's a wrap!" Her daughter, Evie, and Evie's long, swishing ponytail find her in the crowd. Evie grabs her warm-up jacket and her Bible from the bench, and she follows Annie at a distance back to the car.

During the car ride home, they are both silent, listening to local public radio. Annie so tired of this Bible thing, Evie's father recently gifting her one and she is completely against it. Their daughter is too young to consider such ideas, she'll come to it when she's older, she thinks. But, older is now, I guess. Evie taps her fingers haphazardly on the red leather cover of the Bible, and the sound overrides the voices in the speakers, in her head. "Enough," Annie says to her, and Evie looks hurt in a way she wasn't expecting.

Back at home, pitch dark, but still very early evening. Annie looks out to the backyard and sees Evie as a little girl, not even ten years old. She is rubbing up against a tree, the trunk's bark between her legs. She is wearing hot pink stirrup pants. Luckily, Evie has hyper-sensitive hearing. She can hear anyone coming for her from any direction. Snap of branch, stop the heaving. Rustle of leaves, cease the gyration. She remembers feeling a mix of relief and terror: Where did Evie learn the motion? Did she find her xxx videos? Walk in on her unnoticed? Of course not, children figure out pleasure, explore their bodies freely. Annie decided then and there to not embarrass or shame, to talk frank talk using science, facts, but she never did. She doesn't like confrontation.

Annie and Evie's ponytail are eating soggy peas, left-over steak, sticky bread. No complaints from either of them. The telephone bill is on the table. Annie clears her throat and imagines a scenario where she confronts Evie about it, screaming and swearing and name-calling until she is bulging in the neck. Bulging in the neck from yelling is the worst thing she can imagine doing to her.

Another memory: at the doorway of her pink bedroom, Evie is tearing through an encyclopedia, ripping the edges of pages. She can still see the figures of the circulatory system, the muscles shiny, outlined in silver. Annie says, "What are you doing, Evie?" and Evie says "Penis, Ma, I am looking for penis, it was here a few minutes ago and now it's gone. Where is the penis, Ma?" Annie laughs. She was five years old.

The reality is, she thinks, as she watches Evie spill a spoonful of peas onto the floor, missing her mouth, that she could never yell at her beautiful, gangly, young girl with her high blonde ponytail, her gap between her teeth. How can you look at a gap like that, passed down from her father's mother's side, and blame anything on it? You can't, Annie thinks. You cannot do it.

Evie swirls her food around her plate. She looks bored. She grabs the bill. Annie freezes, tries not to make eye contact, can't seem to make her mouth or her hands work. If she could, she would snatch the bill from her hands, tear it to pieces and throw them at her, watch them land on her late, crappy dinner. Accuse her. Punish her. Annie is not the one who called these numbers.

"Ma, are these 1-900 numbers? Like in the back of *Rolling Stone*? The ads with the girls with big boobs? Aren't those illegal?"

Annie can feel the heat rising from somewhere in her chest, into her neck, as if it is ripping through the skin of her face. She meets Evie's big eyes colored full of disappointment.

"Ma, we need to talk." She folds her hands on her lap. "Do you know Jesus Christ as your Lord and Personal Savior?" she asks. "Do you want to?"

₪

Meanwhile, the woman with the red T-shirt that reads DEVOUT PAGAN skips circles around the intersection of curbs, the one way curving at the right angles, as if to say please here look at me, hanging around like a lackadaisical slip under a skirt, lace jerked up a touch. The woman circles, skip turns to gallop, between the DO NOT PARK HERE BETWEEN THE HOURS OF 5 AND 10 PM sign and the YIELD sign, spray-painted over with GET F*CKT in neon green.

There are hours to go before the night will fall on Thick City and you stop hearing the sirens and grid-traffic and the lockjaw. The woman circles, circles. No money, no vice of any kind, no money to buy any vice of any kind.

This is the age to spend the money you make, she thinks. This is the age in which you make the money and you spend it here and there and everywhere you want to. You live in the heart of the city and you spend your money. She sings *Jesus loves the little children, all the children of the world. . .* repeatedly, hopping from one yellow corner to the next, absently watching for cars.

A car with many passengers in it stops in front of MILLIE'S MARKET FINE CUTS, which has been replaced with HIGH LIFE: 1$.00 OTD. A woman with dark hair steps out of the car to the curb, waits for the trunk to pop open, and unloads a stroller. The woman on the corner cannot do anything but stare at the dark-haired woman. She does not jump the curbs, does not finish her perpetual circle, leaves a half-moon, stops singing. The woman picks up a rock off the street, and approaches her.

"Lilith," the woman says. The dark-haired woman's companions are slamming car doors, checking locks, answering phones, folding and putting away. The dark-haired woman shields her eyes from the sun by holding a baby blanket to her forehead, looking out as if she is at sea.

"Adam's first wife," the woman says. The dark-haired woman nods and tips her head back in a fiery laughter, as if she has heard it all before. The woman wraps her fingers tighter around the rock and shoves it into her pocket.

Meanwhile, the kiddie pool full of green Jell-O in the backyard jiggles in the rain. So much of life I don't understand and have never understood, Coley thinks. There are wheat fields out beyond the city walls, flat and unmoving, even in the hardiest of winds. Wheat withstands force in a way few people can. It doesn't simply bend to the will of others, she thinks. R is her new girlfriend. R kisses her forehead, her neck, between her breasts without tenderness. Wheat needs hard shears to cut it down, Coley thinks. She needs to write out all of these thoughts for a new video. R says, "I love you and your dress, thought about you all day after I saw you in it."

In the morning, a light dims and shines on her bedside table. Her phone, unchecked text messages, notifications from the group chat: 57, then 72, then 201. Something has happened in the outside world beyond the city walls. The President of this United States of Ours in Washington D.C. grips the sides of the podium as if her hands will break loose from her body. The sound floats from every screen in America and settles into the rooms where people reckon.

"There is an A side and B side to life," Coley says.

"Isn't the B side mostly duds?" Veronica says.

"No, the B side is the rarest cuts, songs too deep or edgy for the radio," Dani says.

"The B side is right now, here we are. We are in the B side," Annie says.

"No way, this is definitely A side material," Dani says. "Look at the way she grips her podium."

R has left Coley's bed to see another woman, a tall femme with a grown-out mohawk and a wandering eye. She's pretty, but not my type, Coley thinks, and certainly I am jealous for all the wrong reasons. They did not sleep the night before, drink after drink, with R kissing her and telling her how all she can think of is her and the dress. She has not kissed her in weeks.

In the dress. In the dress. Repeating to the point where Coley finally says, "Do you want me to put it back on?" R laughs, slaps her ass. When R left in the middle of the night/early morning, Coley left, too, to the gas station in the opposite direction, to make a video in the car.

The rain is relentless. The wheat beaten down under the violent precipitation, she knows it, she can see it in her third eye. She is dizzy, the room spinny. Her phone buzzes: 201 to 325. Coley deletes the messages without reading them, puts them away.

"Where are you?" Veronica says.

"Do I have to come there?" Dani says.

"What happened last night?" Annie says. "R came by looking like a train wreck."

There is a baby crying through the walls, over the fence, skating along the tops of the fields, out of the city, into the Lake/Ocean far away from her. She lays down in the kiddie pool of green Jell-O. She takes fistfuls and makes a pillow under her head, the weight of her sinks into the gelatin. She shoves some in her mouth and chews.

₪

Meanwhile, we are inside, outside, behind, inside, outside, a dumpster piled high with a man and woman who are lovers/fish. They call themselves spiritual siblings, metaphysical conjoined twins, attached at the fin. Rainbow scales. We are snorting speed from a folded envelope crease, our rat named Wrench perched on our shoulders, cradled in our shirts. The dumpster people/fish are growling about how things are different everywhere, how things have changed, not only in this Thick City, but all over this great big United States of Ours. They nod their heads inside, outside, behind our backs.

Days later, we have returned to our hometown and are mowing our mother's huge dirt lawn, down one side, up another, down one side, up another. She is on her fourth marriage to a fourth fat catfish, every house substantially larger than the last. "Finish line," she says, of many mansions, marriages, catfish. Up one side, down another, wheels stuck in dirt. Huge houses equate to more places to clean in all the various ways one must keep houses clean. "I could do it," she says, "but I don't want to." We offer to be her temporary housekeeper. "How thick," she says, "more house, more shit."

This is the Lake/Ocean shoreline, but here are our dirt dumpsters, more homeless fish sibling-lovers on speed, and it feels like Thick City. After mowing her lawn, we visit an old friend in a side-of-highway motel called the Anchor Inn with no telephones in the rooms and boosted basic cable with one extra, fuzzy, HBO channel. Our old friend is leaving for Vegas in the morning to get away from Thick City. She is using needles these days, bright pink track underbelly. I tell her to maybe lay off the injectables in Vegas, and she gives me a sign of the horns, devil fingers, both hands, heavy metal.

The Great Lake, greatest of all, "sounds like the ocean," our mother says. The waves of the Lake/Ocean sound as if they will overtake the inside of her house even with all the windows shut, a violent flood coming to break us apart.

Sign-of-the-Horns, heavy metal. We flash it in the mirror, more I Love You in sign language than devil music reference. I snap a picture. We are gnashing our teeth. I destroyed the ends of three Bic pens while on the plane here. We can barely speak without having to bite the insides out of our cheeks. When we are back in Thick City, we go see an orthodontist who wants to fit us for a mouthguard to wear when we sleep. Too much speed in envelope creases. We do not have the heart to tell the truth: the speed makes our jaws ache, we grind and clench at night/all the time. We never go back to the orthodontist.

In the seventh floor attic of mother's Lake/Ocean mansion she finds our tackle box full of tinfoil pipes, white-and-black residue. “Are you doing nasty stufffffff? It’ll turn your mouth black!” she yells over the phone. She doesn’t exactly know what “nasty stuff” is, but she knows enough to hang up the phone on us for the first time in our adult lives. So far, since moving to Thick City, when we are tired of adult city life, we have flown back to our hometown, to our mother’s various mansions to rest, but all we are is wet, sharp fish scales in burned-out tinfoil. Needless to say, we are never invited back to our mother’s house.

We think about our hometown all the time. We think about the Lake/Ocean, the suburbs and the cities, boundaries and borders. Thick City. We think about how if speed were legal what would happen to our incisors, or about those dirt twins/lovers in the dumpster a few weeks ago, or the baby in the carriage, or on the other side of the wall. We think about who gets away with what and how. We think about flukes, near misses, direct hits. We think about our Anchor Inn Las Vegas friend and what could happen if she laid off her veins enough to get well. All we can do is dream. We think of heavy metal, what salvation looks like for fishes like us. How the desert, how the money, how the water, gets thinner and thinner inside, outside, behind. How, at any moment, the next draught will be the thing that kills us.

Acknowledgments

Excerpts from *Thick City* have appeared in *Fugue*, *Always Crashing*, and *[PANK]*, sometimes in largely different forms. Many thanks to those editors.

About the Author

Katie Jean Shinkle is the author of four novellas and seven chapbooks, most recently *None of This Is an Invitation* (coauthored with Jessica Alexander, Astrophil Press at University of South Dakota). *Our Prayers after the Fire*, originally published by Blue Square Press, was rereleased by Spuyten Duyvil in 2022. Other work can be found in or is forthcoming from *Flaunt Magazine*, *Denver Quarterly*, *Fugue*, *Witness*, *Crazyhorse*, *Gulf Coast*, and elsewhere. A 2021 Lambda fellow, she serves as co-poetry editor of *DIAGRAM* and teaches in the MFA in Creative Writing, Editing, and Publishing program at Sam Houston State University.

Also by Katie Jean Shinkle

None of This Is an Invitation
Our Prayers after the Fire
The Arson People
Rat Queen
Ruination
Will You Kiss Me Goodnight?